FIVE AT
THE OFFICE
CHRISTMAS
PARTY

Other adventures in this series:

Five Go Gluten Free
Five Go Parenting
Five Go on a Strategy Away Day
Five on Brexit Island
Five Give Up the Booze
Five Forget Mother's Day
Five Lose Dad in the Garden Centre
Five Get Beach Body Ready
Five Get on the Property Ladder
Five Get Gran Online
Five Escape Brexit Island
Five Go Bump in the Night

Enid Blyton

FIVE AT THE OFFICE CHRISTMAS PARTY

Text by
Bruno Vincent

Enid Blyton for Grown-Ups

Quercus

First published in Great Britain in 2017 by

Quercus Editions Ltd
Carmelite House
50 Victoria Embankment
London EC4Y 0DZ

An Hachette UK company

A CIP catalogue record for this book is available
from the British Library

ISBN 978 1 78648 767 4

This book is a work of fiction. Names, characters,
businesses, organizations, places and events are
either the product of the author's imagination
or used fictitiously. Any resemblance to
actual persons, living or dead, events or
locales is entirely coincidental.

Text by Bruno Vincent
Original illustrations by Eileen A. Soper
Cover illustration by Ruth Palmer

10 9 8 7 6 5 4 3 2 1

Typeset by CC Book Production

Printed and bound in Germany by GGP Media GmbH, Pößneck

Contents

CHAPTER ONE

Julian Has an Interview

'Julian?' said the secretary. 'Mr Butler is ready for you.'

'Ah! Yes, of course,' said Julian, jumping up. He fiddled with his tie and nervously shuffled the papers in his hands as the secretary opened the glass door and showed him into the office.

Julian perched on the edge of his seat while the managing director finished his call. He took this opportunity to look out of the floor-to-ceiling glass windows and get a good ogle at the stunning view across the Thames, encompassing the Tower of London, the Tate Modern, the London Eye and, in the distance, the Palace of Westminster.

'Yes, Tim,' said Mr Butler. 'Yes, Tim, I *quite* agree. How clever you are. Ha ha! You old devil. That's why they pay you guys the big bucks, I guess. Speak soon, speak soon. NOW!' Before the handset even landed in the receiver, with the incredible brusqueness of the powerful, Mr Butler's attention was riveted upon Julian.

'Mr Kirrin,' said Butler, looking down at the papers on his desk. 'Good of you to come all the way up.'

Julian nodded towards the window and tried to make an intelligent comment on the view, such as that it was one Canaletto might have painted. But something restricted his vocal chords and all he emitted was a tremulous whine.

'Not at all,' Julian said, when he had his voice under control. 'Thank you for seeing me, and considering my application.'

'Application,' said Mr Butler flatly.

'Y-yes,' said Julian, wondering why it was necessary for the high-ups to keep their offices like saunas. Julian liked to try to give the impression of being confident and imposing. He imagined that was one of the main ways one got ahead in business. When confronted with a man who was genuinely confident and imposing, however, as the managing director certainly was, he found that his confidence had the structural integrity of a sandcastle.

However, he had resolved to get this job, and get this job he certainly would, no matter how much his nervous system sought to undermine him. It was a big step up within the organization, and a career-changing opportunity. He was a strong-willed man of business, he told himself for the thousandth time.

'Ah, yes, your application. I have it here. Very interesting reading.' Mr Butler flicked through it. 'And you've supplied

'Julian?' said the secretary. 'Mr Butler is ready for you.'

an updated CV. Remarkably updated, in fact, from the one you submitted when you joined us.'

'Oh,' said Julian, innocently. 'Are they . . . different?'

'Let's have a look here. So you played tennis in the French Open.'

'That is correct, yes,' said Julian.

'How was that?' asked Mr Butler.

'Oh, fun.'

'Fun, was it? Fun. I see. Let's have another look . . . You've written computer code, and designed a bespoke firewall for your former employer. In what programs do you specialize?'

'MS-DOS,' said Julian confidently.

'Yes, well, I've no idea about those, so I don't know why I asked the question. You spent two years on an underwater geological expedition, mapping the floor of the Marianas Trench.'

'Two and a *half* years.'

'And you attended Tokyo Business School.'

'Indeed.'

'*Kuchoma nguruwe korodani*?'

'That's the one,' said Julian.

'I *see*,' said Mr Butler. 'Mr Kirrin, I'm a busy man, and quite frankly I've already had enough of this.'

'Yes,' said Julian, 'perhaps we could move on to my ideas

for innovation in the department, and why I am a strong candid—'

'We shall do no such thing,' said Mr Butler. 'I did not invite you here to discuss this appalling tissue of fabrications, although I admit it did afford me a small amount of amusement.'

'No?' asked Julian distantly.

'No. You see, there is another candidate for the job. A *genuinely* strong candidate. And I shall be giving the job to him. You sit next to him, I believe. A Mr David Masterman?'

The tremulous whine took up residence once more in Julian's throat.

'Yes,' he said. 'Well, I'm afraid, if you listen to a word that man says . . .'

'Then it is hard not to form a certain picture of *you*, Kirrin. It appears Mr Masterman has had to put up with a great deal.'

'Not at all; it's the other way round. He smells—'

'He most certainly does not. It is you, Mr Kirrin, who regularly come into work with bloodshot eyes and reeking of alcohol,' said the M.D.

'Perhaps my aftershave contains some,' said Julian. 'I do splash it on a bit.'

'I can see from here you have not shaved in many days,' said Mr Butler. 'You have also, since being moved to sit next to Mr Masterman, placed a drawing pin on his chair, for him to sit on, on a daily basis.'

'Not me,' said Julian. 'Not me.'

'When he is on the phone to clients, you repeat what he's saying in a whiny voice.'

'I'm trying to help him,' said Julian. 'To help him learn how annoying he is. So he can grow.'

'When he leaves his computer unlocked, you go on to his machine and send emails to people from his account, saying things like . . .' He examined the paper on the desk in front of him. '"I'm a smelly poohead"; "My name is Dr Whiffy", and so on.'

'He *is* a smelly poohead,' said Julian. 'I suspect it is a manifestation of his subconscious.'

'Do you know what sort of men I employ, Mr Kirrin?'

'Confident ones,' Julian said. He'd rehearsed this bit. 'Talented, committed, innovators and leaders.'

'That is correct. Do you know what sort of men I do not employ?'

'No?'

'Worms.'

'Worms?'

'Worms. Do you know what we do with worms?'

'Feed . . . them . . . ?'

'We crush them.'

'Yes, I suppose you do.'

'You, Kirrin, are a worm. Now, exit this building at once, before I crush you.'

'I see,' said Julian.

'One more thing,' said Mr Butler, who had replaced his spectacles and was already dialling a new number. 'What I said to you just now was not the name of the Tokyo Business College. I asked you whether you wanted roasted pig testicles.'

'I see,' said Julian.

'In Swahili.'

'Right,' said Julian. 'Well, I must say, they sound very similar.'

'Good day,' said Mr Butler.

It occurred to Julian that, if he was going to think of something clever to say in order to make a grand exit, now would be the moment. He looked at Mr Butler.

'Bye,' he said. And went out, closing the door behind him.

He stumbled into the street somewhat dazed, before realizing he'd left his jacket on the back of the chair at his desk. But the security guard would no longer allow him into the building.

As Julian walked down the street, the heavens opened,

7

'You, Kirrin, are a worm. Now leave before I crush you.'

and without a tree in sight to shelter beneath, he simply trudged along through the rain. Taking his phone out, he dialled George.

'Bad news,' he said. 'I got fired. I'm going to have to get another job.'

'Worse news,' said George. 'There's a job going here. At the seat between me and Anne. Send your C.V. over.'

'It'll take some editing,' said Julian.

'Just send it, dickhead.' She rang off.

Having skipped breakfast owing to nerves over the big interview, Julian felt his stomach rumble. He wondered what roasted pig testicles actually tasted like.

CHAPTER TWO

Five Go to Work

So it was that Julian came to join George, Anne and Dick working at the firm of their notoriously shady cousin, Rupert. They knew very little about what the business did, exactly, only that they were in need of work and that Rupert had been kind enough to offer them some. It was of the lowest, data-entry kind, but they were grateful nonetheless.

Julian had only been there for a week, but they had already settled into a certain routine.

Each morning, Anne got up early to go for a run, then returned, knocked on Dick's door to wake him, showered, ate some fruit and yoghurt, and stood in front of the mirror, needlessly augmenting her immaculate appearance for forty minutes.

During this time, George staggered out of her room, pulling on a jumper and jeans, poured a scoop of muesli into a bowl, splashed milk on it, crunched one mouthful, made a face and threw it away. Then she slung her record bag over her shoulder, attached her helmet and lights, and left on her bike.

Anne reappeared from her room looking wonderful and knocked on Dick's door again, and then on Julian's. She ignored the indignant shouts from within and set off for the Tube station.

Dick would then appear, looking zombie-like, go to the bathroom and splash water on his face and under his armpits, dry both vigorously, spray himself with cheap corner-shop deodorant and then set about preparing his and Julian's breakfast. This was a very special recipe, arrived at over years of experimentation, and it could not vary in even the tiniest detail.

For each sandwich, two sausages were first cooked on the George Foreman Grill, during which time Dick made coffee. The cooked sausages were then sliced in half lengthways and placed on a slice of bread, above a layer of mild Cheddar cheese (which melted with a far more pleasing consistency than the mature kind). Over the top of the sausages was smeared a layer of peanut butter, on to which were sprinkled finely chopped spring onions and green chilli. A final layer of ketchup (brand not stipulated) was added, and a second slice of bread was placed on top. The resultant sandwich was then placed on the grill until the telltale sizzle of molten cheese could be heard.

This sandwich (which Julian regarded as the finest achievement of Western civilization since Mahler's Fifth Symphony) was actually a bit much for Dick at breakfast. Usually, he had one bite and then wrapped it in foil for lunch. Leaving coffee in the pot for Julian, he'd get dressed in two minutes, then (most days) remember to brush his teeth, before wandering off down the street whistling and listening to dubstep on his oversized headphones.

The slam of the door as Dick left usually caused Julian to wake with a start, and stare about him. Then he would turn on Radio 4 and doze for ten minutes before realizing he wasn't listening to the *Today* programme, but something else. Which meant it was after nine. Meaning he'd be late *again*. With a roar of self-loathing, he would leap out of bed, scurry to the bathroom and perform his ablutions, which invariably involved a brief pause when, remembering the final drink or two from the night before, he fixed himself with a furious look in the mirror.

'It's *you*!' he would cry. 'It's always you! Why do you do this to me! *Come* on, Julian!'

Invigorated by this condensed version of the Two Minutes Hate, he would dress quickly, take a scalding swig of the coffee straight from the jug because he thought it was the sort of thing Hemingway would have done, cough splutteringly

Now he had been put in charge,
Julian's respect for the rights of the working man
seemed to mysteriously melt away.

over the sink for a few moments, and leave with the reliably splendid sausage sandwich in his hands.

The sandwich he dealt with in four large bites, thinking all the while how much he loved his younger brother. One day, he thought. One day I will have the chance to make it up to that guy. He's saved my life again . . .

The routine might have been comforting, but the work they were heading for was positively dreary. So it's perfectly understandable that, most mornings, each of them had the idle fantasy of some sort of accident preventing them from reaching the office.

Anne was a sensible young woman with a knack for organization. Therefore, her fantasy was not only efficient but involved multitasking. It included some sort of slight malfunction with the Tube train, which led to them being stuck in the tunnel for hours, and then being led to safety by a confident, courteous and well-dressed young man, whose father (conversation would reveal) had a country seat, and was extremely elderly . . .

Dick envisaged being run over by a cyclist or getting a brief glancing blow from a cab. Just the right amount to knock him off his feet – he could do the rest. He would exaggerate the pain to his G.P. and wangle six weeks off or so. Enough to really get to grips with *Legend of Zelda* on the Nintendo Switch. Untrammelled bliss . . .

George was not a morning person. Her fantasy, therefore, had a decidedly more apocalyptic tone. She hated being bored more than anything – and she hated lots of things. The job they were doing was the most boring she'd ever done, by some considerable distance. The fantasy she entertained, as she turned the corner towards the offices each morning, was that the building would be struck by an out-of-control vehicle – a large one, such as a speeding fire engine, or (better) a petrol tanker – which would explode, demolishing the whole block. Variations on this included the office being struck by a meteorite or disappearing into a sinkhole. She didn't envision any of her colleagues (aside from her cousins, of course) having a chance to escape, and so presumably they were all destroyed along with the building – she really didn't mind one way or the other. It eased the burden of reaching work, just a tiny bit.

Julian's fantasy was far more vainglorious. In his version, he stumbled across a terrorist attack, which he single-handedly foiled while hundreds of bystanders cowered, screaming. He imagined receiving some sort of cosmetic injury (a bullet wound to the shoulder, perhaps, or a facial scar), and then possibly taking out one of the offenders in a violent and dramatic way.

There would be video footage, of course. The sight of him knocking a terrorist's block off would feature on the evening news, the next day's newspapers and YouTube. He would be known worldwide as the Hero of London, and prove devastatingly self-deprecating in interviews. He would be invited on talk shows and would be so funny he was invited to guest host *Have I Got News For You*. Think how it would affect his stock with the young women of London . . . never formerly very high . . . The mind boggled . . .

By now, he would usually start to nod over his Eric Ambler novel, miss his stop, and have to catch a Tube back in the other direction.

CHAPTER THREE

The Resource Realignment Project

The office building that filled them with such dread was on a characterless, nondescript side street in King's Cross, with stunted and unhappy-looking trees growing out of the pavement every fifty yards.

There was an understanding among the housemates that they would under no circumstances speak to each other on the way to work even if, by some freak of chance or alteration to routine, they crossed paths.

The commute was the only time in the day one truly had to oneself. Julian used it for reading, George for catching up on podcasts, Dick for improving his high score on *Candy Crush* and, when there was elbow space on the Tube, Anne liked to knit, while listening to a language course on her phone.

Each Kirrin youngster checked in with their key card and stood yawning in the lift to the third floor. The third floor was considered somewhat glamorous by the benighted inhabitants of the ground, first and second floors, but was looked upon with chuckling condescension by those who worked higher up the building.

The first three arrived in dribs and drabs, but Julian was always last in. When they reached their desks, they said hello in a cheerful and friendly way, as though they hadn't spoken since five thirty p.m. the previous day.

'What does today hold?' Julian would ask loudly and cheerfully, to a general silence. Dick went to make coffee for them all, while Anne got straight on with her work with high energy and George looked at her screen dismally, tapping a key now and then.

Julian didn't mind the repetitive work. For one, he was grateful to be in employment again so soon after what he regarded as his recent little misunderstanding with Mr Butler. Also, he tended to furiously overthink every task he was given, so, for Julian, data entry was a rather soothing occupation.

Making the morning coffee, Dick tended to linger in the kitchen, not to escape work (for Dick did no work, none at all, not a stroke), but because he got to say hello to colleagues, one by one. He supposed he liked them, in a vague sort of way, but he certainly found them entertaining.

First in was usually Suze, a woman in her mid-forties with bleached-blond hair, who smiled a great deal when she was face to face with you, but whose face very obviously fell back into its customary mask of dread the instant she turned away, as though she thought once out of eye contact, she was invisible. She talked with gleeful horror about the behaviour of her grown-up children, who seemed to be getting up to all sorts of borderline-illegal activities.

Usually, she came in just as Dick was about to plunge the cafetière, causing him to dally while she fetched herself a cup of tea, into which she poured sugar from the packet (to a measure, Dick estimated conservatively, of about eight teaspoons), while talking about last night's TV and laughing loudly at her own remarks.

Today was different, however. Suze looked haggard.

'Have you heard about the redundancies?' she asked.

'No,' Dick said. 'What redundancies?'

'They're gonna sack a lot of us. Just heard. Don't tell anyone. God, I hope it isn't me. They'll pick Ken, I bet. Good luck, Julian.'

Dick nodded thoughtfully while he plunged the coffee, not bothering to correct her about his name.

As Dick was laying out the cups, into the kitchen strode Jim Granger. He was tall and straight-backed, which made his stomach stick out, and he never removed his jacket. He was perhaps just past fifty-five, and wore an expression of studied world-weariness, as though he wanted no one to be under any illusion that he hadn't seen it all before.

'Morning, young man,' he said. 'Have you heard the news?'

'About the redundancies?' Dick asked.

Jim Granger (for some reason, no one ever just called him Jim) looked startled. 'Keep your voice down, lad, you'll scare the horses. Who told you?'

'Naming no names,' said Dick, pouring out the coffee. But he instinctively cast a glance down the corridor in the direction Suze had just disappeared.

'Oh, her,' said Jim Granger. 'Well, she'll be sure to go. Good riddance. If you don't pull your weight, then you can sling your hook.'

'Because it's a dog-eat-dog world?' Dick asked.

'I've taught you well, young man,' said Jim Granger, smiling complacently. Dick felt a slimy coil of disgust wriggle in his belly.

'It's not redundancies, by the way,' Jim Granger went on. 'They're calling it the Resource Realignment Project. Obviously, lots of people are screwed, but I'm glad to say that I'm not going to be one of them. Not Jim Granger.'

'No?' asked Dick. 'Sorry, I mean: no.'

'*No*,' said Jim Granger. 'I've heard that lots of people are

Most mornings, each of them had the idle fantasy of some sort of accident preventing them from reaching the office.

going to get moved around. Some – Ken, I expect – to the Daventry office. Never to be seen again, if you know what I mean.'

'Well, of course,' said Dick. 'They'd move there.'

'No, you dolt – I mean fired. Let go.'

'Oh,' said Dick. 'That seems a shame.'

'That's the world, mate,' said Jim Granger, with relish. 'Listen, if anyone asks about you, I'll stand up for you. I like you. You're a *hard worker*. Like me. There's no flies on you, Julian. See you later, lad.'

Dick smiled wanly as Jim Granger left. Then he cast his eyes over the noticeboard, on which was posted a leaflet about a charity cake sale the following month, a request for someone to '*PLEASE return Ken's stapler (sentimental value)*' and several out-of-date vouchers for local businesses.

'Hullo, Dick,' said a sad voice.

'Oh, hey, mate!' said Dick. Aside from the pleasant surprise of someone getting his name right, here was a person he genuinely liked. 'How you doing, Ken?'

'Dying slowly,' said Ken. He shuffled to the sink and began washing out his mug. 'Too slowly, really. Could do with it speeding up a bit.'

'Stapler still missing?'

Ken nodded. 'Think I need some caffeine.'

'Come on, you miserable git,' said Dick, punching him in the arm. 'There's plenty more staplers in the, er . . . the stationery-cupboard . . . sea.'

'Don't do that to metaphors, Dick,' Ken said. 'What have they ever done to you?'

Ken was a heavily acne-scarred twenty-five-year-old who was obviously and profoundly depressed. He had sandy blond hair and a pained expression. He was intelligent, wry and had good taste in music, film and books. He was the ideal pub quiz companion, in fact, and the Kirrins all liked him enormously.

'Cheer up, you big bastard,' said Dick, as he poured milk into the coffees, and Ken brewed himself a tea. 'Or I'll kick you in the balls.'

'That would provide a welcome distraction from this morning's progress meeting, for which I would be grateful,' said Ken reflectively, 'but then it would also be excruciatingly painful. Can life get any better? Oh, yes: I was forgetting the Resource Realignment Project.'

'So you've heard?' Dick asked, returning the milk to the fridge.

'Of course I've heard,' Ken said. 'Who told you?'

'Suze. Jim Granger knows, too.'

'He'll be the first to go,' Ken said. 'If that blonde cow he's shagging doesn't beat him out the door.'

'This gossip is above my pay grade,' said Dick. 'Ken, you're, ah ... you're being refreshingly indiscreet. Is he really? I mean, are they?'

'At it like jackhammers,' said Ken. 'But then like attracts like, so the incompetent and the pointless are naturally drawn to each other.'

'Like you and me?' said Dick.

'Exactly,' said Ken. 'I'll be online in fifteen minutes.'

'Bang on it, mate,' said Dick. 'See you then.'

He took the coffees back to the desks of his brother, sister and cousin, and handed them out. Then he sat and when no one was looking, logged on to his online game with Ken.

'Chin-chin, you big bloody lifesaver,' said Julian, taking a swig. Again neglecting to check how scalding the coffee was, he made a face like someone with their arm caught in a tractor. His eyes rolled in their sockets as he waited for the pain to recede.

'Any news from the break-out beverage area?' asked Anne, as she tapped away.

'Just that we're all getting fired,' said Dick.

Julian spat his coffee all over his keyboard.

CHAPTER FOUR

A Special Assignment

'Now, I suppose you're wondering why I've gathered you all here today,' said Rupert.

'Not at all. We know. It's to fire us, you disloyal bastard!' shouted Julian.

'Thank you, Penny. That's lovely. No, there will be nothing else; you can go.' Rupert smoothed his tie as his secretary exited the room and closed the door.

'Well, now, you might have waited until we were alone before you aired this unfounded grievance,' Rupert said placidly.

'Unfounded, is it?' asked Julian, standing up. 'Prove it!'

'Of *course* I can prove it,' said Rupert. 'We're in a meeting expressly to discuss my plans for you lot.'

'Well, then,' said Julian, sitting back down. He felt like he'd roughly made his point, and was oblivious to the acrid stares he was receiving from the others.

Rupert, perfectly unfazed, went on as though he hadn't been interrupted.

There was an understanding among the housemates that they would under no circumstances speak to each other on the way to work.

'NOW. I've got a proper job for you . . .'

'Huh. How long will that last?' muttered Julian.

'Shut up, Julian,' said Anne. 'Rupert. We're so grateful for you giving us any work at all. Please, go on.'

'As you may know, we've recently initiated a crucial restructuring process in the company.'

'Yes,' said Dick. 'It does seem to be on many people's horizons.'

'They all seem rather concerned,' said Anne.

'It's fucking them up like no one's business,' said George.

'An unfortunate effect of complex reorganizations like this,' said Rupert. 'And no one feels it harder than me.'

The four examined his pained countenance closely to see if they could detect the disingenuousness that they knew lay beneath. As always, with Rupert, they were frustrated – he was a study in humane grief.

'Which is why I've brought you here,' he said. 'There's a project.'

'The Resource Realignment Project,' said Julian, still simmering with disgust.

'Julian,' said Rupert, 'sometimes companies have to restructure themselves in order to keep going. It might seem senseless and brutal to you . . .'

'Correct.'

'. . . but the alternative is that everyone would lose their jobs. Which is, of course, appalling. Rather than go through redundancies, we are looking at altering our business to help everyone as much as we can.'

'Oh, you are *good*,' said Anne, with feeling.

'Some will move to a higher floor,' said Rupert. 'Some will move to the basement. Some will be moved to the Chigwell office. Some may, unfortunately, have to be let go. But that's where you come in.'

'We won't help you in the dreadful culling of these innocent victims!' Julian cried. 'Workers' rights!'

'Did you not stand as a Conservative M.P. at the last election?' Rupert asked.

'Youthful foolishness,' said Julian. 'I've grown out of it.'

'Well, good for you. But I assure you there'll be no culling involved in the job I'm tasking you.'

'Is "tasking" a verb now?' asked Julian.

'Oh, SHUT UP!' said the other three. And, had Timmy been there, there would undoubtedly have been a disapprobatory 'woof' as well.

Julian realized he was standing up and pointing, and that there was even a fleck of spittle on his lips. Perhaps he was overreacting a tad. Wiping his mouth with his sleeve, he sat down.

'As I said, I have,' Rupert went on, 'a job for you. While the RRP is in train, I appreciate that the morale in the office may take a bit of a dip. It's only natural – and we must do what we can to keep people's spirits up. Therefore, what I want you to do is to organize a really great office Christmas party.'

He suddenly had their attention. They looked at each other. That sounded . . . well, almost fun.

'You can come up with ideas, research venues and so forth, and get the whole thing planned. Come December sixteenth, I need you to have a party ready that's merry and cheerful and different, to cheer the whole company up.'

'What about the data-entry work?' Anne asked.

'Oh, don't worry about that. It's a rolling project that will take years to complete. It's the party that I want you to concentrate on. Do you think you can do it?'

'I know we can!' said Julian. Straightaway he could see some incredibly appealing perks. 'We're the ones for the job!'

'Good. I thought as much. Now, I'm giving you a decent budget: fifteen hundred pounds. And we'll cover all your expenses – just give receipts to Penny at the end of each month and we'll put what you spend in your wages, so you're not out of pocket.'

'What a nice challenge – thank you, Rupert,' said Anne.

'Yeah,' said George. 'Sounds all right.'

'No, thank *you*,' said Rupert. 'Now if you will excuse me, I must take a most pressing call.' As they got out of their chairs Rupert pressed a button and the large screen on the wall behind his desk blinked on. On it was a video of what looked like a disused warehouse, in the centre of which was a man tied to a chair with ropes. His face was bruised and blood from his nose trickled over the tape that covered his mouth. Rupert hurriedly stabbed at the remote control in his hand and the image disappeared.

'Is that . . .' Dick asked suspiciously. 'Is that the new Liam Neeson film?'

'Yes,' said Rupert. 'Liam Neeson. Yes it is.' Then he pressed a button on his deskphone. 'Penny, could you come in here and help me with the controls to this thing? Thank you. So long, cousins.'

They got up and left the office.

'Nearly lunchtime,' said Anne. 'Can I fetch you anything from Pret?'

'Bugger Pret,' said Julian. 'We've got research to do!'

CHAPTER FIVE

Research This!

'Julian,' said Anne, 'I just don't see that it would be appropriate to have an office Christmas party in a Chinese restaurant.'

Julian gasped as he pushed away his empty plate.

'You know what? I tend to agree,' he said, loosening his belt and shifting his chair back from the table. 'But I just wanted to *check*.' He gulped down the remains of his green tea.

Anne had rather pecked at her food, but George and Dick were in a similar state of torpor to Julian. They stared glassily at the bowls arrayed in front of them, which contained the last traces of red-cooked pork, barbecue ribs, choi sum in oyster sauce, lamb with cumin seeds, fish-fragrant aubergines and chicken with black beans. Beside these stood a leaning tower of empty dim sum steamers.

'Urg,' said Dick.

'Come on, we'd best get back,' said Anne.

'To what?' said George.

'It's our job to be out here, researching,' said Julian. 'If we went back, we'd be attempting to do our job remotely, from *within* the office. Which is ridiculous. Now, when we're able to move, I'd like to try out another place, a little way across town . . .'

'Excuse me,' said Anne. 'I'm sorry to bother you, but I was wondering whether you ever have parties here?'

'Party? Of course!' said the Italian man behind the counter. 'How old is child?'

'No, sorry – I mean, for adults.'

'Adults?'

'Yes, an office party. In the evening.'

The man looked confused and annoyed. 'No, never. We don't do.'

Anne looked at Julian with triumph.

'I told you this was madness,' she said.

'Too late!' said Julian, turning away from the counter with a tray in his hand. On it were several coffees and three rather superb ice-cream sundaes, each frilled with whipped cream and drooling with sauce.

'I got a chocolatey one, a fruity one and a toffee-butter-scotchy one,' he said, plonking the tray on the table.

Dick and George tucked in at once.

'While the project is in train, I appreciate that the morale in the office may take a bit of a dip.'

'I think this is rather irresponsible,' said Anne. 'Did you get one for me?'

'I got you a spoon. They're for sharing. Have a bit of each, get stuck in – it's research.'

Anne brushed one of the ice creams with the tip of her spoon and then touched it to her tongue. 'Mmm,' she said.

'There we go,' said Julian. 'Get a wodge of this stuff down your neck. It's quality. Woof!'

'I wish Timmy was here,' said George.

'It's a perfectly ridiculous idea to try and have an office party at a gelateria,' Anne said through a mouthful of cream, 'and you knew that all along, Julian.'

'Exploring all avenues,' he said.

'Maybe I will bring Timmy in tomorrow; I hate leaving him at home,' George said. 'God, I *love* this butterscotch one.'

'I mean, this place is only big enough for about eight people. It'd be impossible to fit everyone from the office in, anyway,' Anne went on. 'Even if they did Christmas parties, which they don't.'

'What can I say?' replied Julian. 'I'm learning on the job. The fruity sorbet one's good too, George. Tuck in . . .'

Wandering back towards the office, the four took a wrong turn and found themselves on a backstreet outside a large pub, in the window of which they noticed a sign boasting of the large function hall at the rear. It was no more than ten minutes away from the office, and even Anne couldn't deny that it was a very decent contender for the party venue.

They went inside, and while they waited for the landlord to come down from upstairs to talk to them, Julian asked if anyone wanted a drink.

'I'll have a sparkling water, thank you,' said Anne.

The others paused. They were still in work time. They were technically *at* work. But as they'd had a large and profoundly satisfying lunch, followed by coffee and a delicious dessert, naturally their bodies were crying out for a little digestif.

Julian decided to steamroller over the awkwardness.

'Session ales for me and Dick,' he said. 'George?'

'Yeah,' she said, 'I think I could handle a little vee and tee.'

The barman arrived with Anne's sparkling mineral water.

'Actually,' Anne said, smiling sweetly, 'would you mind putting a small white wine in that? Thanks ever so.'

The landlord showed them through to the hall at the back. He told them the prices and talked them through the sort of parties the space was normally hired for. It did indeed seem pretty suitable, and he was certainly interested in their

35

business. He offered them another drink as they sat down to talk through the details. It seemed churlish to refuse.

When he disappeared off on an errand, the four housemates still had most of their drinks left. So they searched among the board games on the shelf and were soon engrossed in a game of Buckaroo!.

'No point going back to the office now,' said Julian, when they had finished their drinks. 'Anyone want another pint of research?'

They all nodded.

CHAPTER SIX

Julian Clicks Reply

Dear Suze, Julian wrote. *I'm glad that you're happy the toner in the photocopier has been changed. However, we don't all need to receive an email telling us this fact. Could you possibly take care not to press the 'Reply All' button? We all send and receive hundreds of emails each day* (this was a lie; Julian received hardly any, and frequently checked his inbox with disappointment) *and so, if we could keep the number of unnecessary communications to a minimum, it would honestly help all our lives.*

Julian looked around the office and sighed. He felt dreadful. But then, so did the others. Seeing it was nearly eleven o'clock, as a practised hangover survivor, he knew it was almost time for the run to the shops for crisps, biscuits, fizzy drinks and Alka-Seltzer. However, before that, he wanted to get this email just right – he was always touchy on a hangover and Suze's message had tipped him over the edge.

To be honest with you, he typed on, *I don't really under-stand why you would press 'Reply All' in the first place. I mean no disrespect, but did you honestly think it would benefit the other (several hundred) employees to receive a message from you reading, simply, 'Yaaay'? One might almost say it shows you do not think about the result of your actions, which is risky behaviour in front of your manager, I would suggest.*

Julian was aware that he had plenty of actual work to get on with. But, reading back what he had written, he felt a twitch of irritation. Warming to his theme, he couldn't help but continue.

I assume that there must be some sort of decision-making process in your brain when you go to press 'Reply All'. One does have to deliberately press it, after all. Is it to get attention? Or a cry for help?

Do you imagine that the people who receive your email laugh, or smile? That your happy-go-lucky attitude brings a moment of light into their otherwise grey lives? I'm sorry to say, the reality is the opposite. It makes people hate you. It makes them grind their teeth, and sigh, and despair, and visualize you being thrown to a pack of ravening hounds to have the flesh torn from your body to the tune of your gargling screams.

Julian deleted the last two paragraphs, sighed again, picked up his coffee and went to take a sip. But he hesitated. Twice bitten, third time shy, he thought. Blow on it first, he thought,

Julian realized he must have clicked Reply All.
'Balls,' he said quietly.

make sure it's cool enough to drink. As he lowered his mouth to do so, the air was torn by a devastatingly loud and high-pitched howl that jolted him in his seat and emptied half the hot coffee into his lap.

He flailed wildly and clutched his chest as his breathing started to return. Then he patted his thighs, desperately trying to ease the burn. Glancing around, he saw everyone else working on as before, undisturbed. Looking at his screen, he saw it was eleven a.m. Of course.

'Does he really have to test that fire alarm *every single pissing* day?' Julian roared.

Returning from the toilets, fifteen minutes later, with most of the coffee rinsed out of his trousers and most of the water dried away, Julian read through his email to Suze again. Hangover, shock, embarrassment and anger had now joined forces to form an intense above-the-temples throb. Satisfying himself that all of the actually rude material had come out while the tone remained potently aggressive, he clicked send.

'Hah,' said George, beside him. 'That's funny.'

'What is?' he asked.

'Your email.'

'*What*?'

Julian looked back at his inbox to find it filling with out-of-offices – first six of them, then a dozen, then two dozen – the identical subject line that had annoyed him in the first place, repeated over and over until it filled up his screen. They were coming from all around the building, and from the company's other offices across the world – Caracas, Johannesburg, Adelaide. Julian realized he must have clicked *Reply All*.

'Balls,' he said quietly.

CHAPTER SEVEN

Reporting Group

Although they had already been scouting for locations, it wasn't until the following Friday that the Christmas Party Reporting Group had their first official catch-up meeting in the office, in order to share ideas and research. Having been placed in charge of the group, and appointed (after repeatedly pressing Rupert for a job title) Seasonal Social Executive Vice President, Julian had found that his ardent support of the rights of the working man started to mysteriously melt away. He now referred to his cousins as his 'underlings', even when they were in the flat, and regarded their every deed with a mixture of paranoia, impatience and scorn.

Most of the inaugural party-planning session had been taken up with agreeing the aforementioned name for the group. This monumental task achieved, they broke for coffee.

'Erm, could we get a little further down the agenda before we break?' Julian asked. 'Sorry to be a bore . . .'

'Union rules,' Dick said. 'We're allowed a coffee and a biscuit in any meeting that goes on for an hour.'

'You've joined a union?' Julian asked.

'We've been here an *hour*?' said George, waking up.

'Okay, fine, fine – dish out the hot drinks and the Hobnobs, and then we'll get back to it . . .'

'Has anyone been watching *Fargo*?' Dick asked.

'Oh! Has the new series started?' asked Anne.

'Yeah, it's looking pret—'

'Seriously, let's get on with this,' said Julian.

'You can't break union rules, mate,' said Dick. 'There will be ramifications.'

'The ramifications,' said Julian, 'if you use being in a union to delay this meeting any longer, will be that I come into your room in the night and sit on your neck.'

Dick sipped his coffee and nibbled his biscuit, muttering something about the brutal oppression of the labour force, while Julian tried to get the meeting back on track.

'So,' said Julian. 'Give me your ideas.'

'First,' said George, 'no mention of Christmas.'

'Hmm,' said Julian. 'I'm sorry, what did you say?'

'It's discriminatory to those of different faiths,' said George. 'No Christmas.'

'We've been put in charge of the Christmas party and literally the first thing you try to do is to cancel Christmas?' asked Julian.

Three weeks later, the Christmas Party Reporting Group were waiting somewhat nervously outside Rupert's door.

'Stop living in the past,' George said. 'You can't call it Christmas anymore. Anyone in this office might be Jewish, or Muslim, or Buddhist. Or Chinese.'

'What on earth do you mean they *might* be Chinese?'

'How would you feel if you were working in a Chinese company and they only celebrated Chinese New Year, and not Christmas?'

'Fine. I'd be fine about it,' said Julian. 'Excited!'

'Christmas is out. We should call it the Midwinter Festival Party.'

'Let's talk about it later,' said Julian. 'Let's move on to the next item on the agenda: food. We've got to have some food, right? To soak up the booze. Stop people getting too wrecked.'

'That's another thing,' said George. 'No booze.'

'George?' Julian asked. 'Have I done something to upset you?'

'Me?' asked George. 'No?'

'Then why are you trying to ruin my life?'

'I'm trying to improve it,' said George. 'Yours and everyone's. I've been reading up about this and apparently workforces are actively harmed when they consume alcohol together. It leads to embarrassment, inappropriate behaviour, consequent long-lasting inhibition and ruined relationships. It damages the company.'

'This meeting is adjourned,' said Julian. Then he gathered his wallet and, saying he had an external appointment, went out to the pub.

CHAPTER EIGHT

Goodbye, Dear Colleague

Towards the end of the afternoon, Ken came round to the desks of the four housemates, looking somewhat apologetic.

'Thought you might like to sign Rog's card,' said Ken.

Anne, George and Dick did it without thinking, but Julian paused.

'Good old Rog,' said Julian. 'Er . . . Forgive me – which one's he again?'

Ken seemed crestfallen. 'W-well,' he stammered, 'I really wouldn't like to say.'

'Give me a clue,' said Julian.

'He's sort of a bit . . . No, I really can't say,' said Ken.

'All right, all right, I take it he's the one with the gammy leg,' said Julian. 'Hand the card over.'

Ken paused for a long time, staring at Julian. Then he slowly handed the card over.

What to write?

'I don't know the guy,' said Julian, frustrated. 'What's he like? Oh, forget it; I'll just write something nice.'

Snatching a pen off his desk, Julian scrawled in a big, friendly, looping hand, *HAPPY BIRTHDAY, ROG! 21 AGAIN, EH, HA HA! HAVE A GREAT ONE, MATE!* He signed it with a kiss, assuming that such expressions of affection between males were no longer regarded with suspicion in this day and age. He gave it back to Ken, who stared at it with horror.

'It's his leaving card,' he said.

'Oh, fuck,' said Julian, 'is it? Why didn't you tell me?'

'It's on the front of the card,' said Ken. 'And if you look at all the other messages . . .'

'All right, all right,' said Julian. 'Well, er . . . Give me a minute . . .'

Working as fast as he could, and trying to ignore Ken's mordant stare, Julian performed a botched rescue operation on the card, which consisted of layers of Tipp-Ex and lots more biro. When he handed it back, ten minutes later, Ken looked at it with disappointment. It now resembled a piece of art by an unusually ham-fisted six-year-old.

'Sorry,' said Julian. 'Here. Have a tenner.'

Ken looked startled.

'For the collection,' Julian said.

Ken nodded, and then limped away.

Ah, Julian thought. So Rog *isn't* the one with the gammy leg.

Food was agreed on: pies, sandwiches, sausage rolls,
Scotch eggs. Cake, trifle, jelly and ice cream.

CHAPTER NINE

The Christmas Party Reporting Group's Christmas Party Report

Three weeks later, the Christmas Party Reporting Group were waiting somewhat nervously outside Rupert's door. At length, Penny gestured for them to enter.

'Team!' said Rupert warmly, as they came into his office. 'How good to see you. Come in, sit down. You don't mind if I carry on with this?'

'Er, n-no . . .' stuttered Anne.

They found their chairs laid out in a fan formation in front of Rupert, who was in sweats, sprinting on a treadmill.

'Señor Keerin!' said a miserable voice. 'No delivery! Stolen by *bandidos*!'

Rupert quickly tapped a button on the console.

'Just a minute, Ricardo; thought I'd taken you off speaker-phone. Now, don't you worry. I'll talk to our Russian friend and make sure he knows the consequences if he lets us down. Your villagers will have their medicine.'

He paused. 'Your "*villagers*", I said . . . No, "*medicine*". I was speaking in – never mind. I've got to go.'

He tapped another button on the control pad and then turned his confident smile towards the four housemates.

'So, where are we on this Christmas party?' he asked. 'Hoping we're looking at a really strong plan. Only ten days to go, after all. If I can send out an announcement today, hopefully everyone will be excited – I know I am. So?'

Before outlining the plan, Julian explained their thinking, and how they'd come to their decisions, to give Rupert the impression they'd been firing on all cylinders and exploring every conceivable option.

Rupert nodded along – at least, they thought he did; it was hard to tell while he was running. He seemed to be doing interval training, meaning that he frequently sprinted for a few minutes, pounding the treadmill hard and gasping for breath, his face in a rictus that might have been a grin or a mask of pain. He also checked his emails throughout on an iPad attached to his forearm by a Velcro strip, which made it even harder to tell if he was listening.

Aside from these distractions, however, by the end, it seemed as though Rupert had taken it all in, and didn't seem disgusted with their findings. In fact, once Julian had finished his report, Rupert even slowed the treadmill to a stop in order to give them feedback. Either that, or his workout had finished.

'Sounds great,' he said, towelling his hair. 'Go ahead.'

'Great,' said Julian. 'I'm so relieved. After you put your trust in us, I can't deny I was anxious to do a good job.'

'Which you've done,' said Rupert, over his shoulder, going towards the door to his executive bathroom. 'So book it.'

'Yes,' said Julian, slightly surprised the conversation seemed to be at an end. He still wanted reassurance on one point. 'But they need a deposit.'

Rupert paused, holding the bathroom door open. For the first time since they'd all been children together, the house-mates saw him laugh.

'Use the budget. I gave you a budget, Julian! Fifteen hundred pounds.'

In response to this, Julian also laughed, but it was a far less pleasant and relaxing sound. 'But that was the *research* budget,' he said.

Rupert allowed the door to swing shut, and walked back towards them. Julian looked left and right.

'The what, did you say?' Rupert said.

'The research budget,' Julian repeated. 'Surely.'

'A separate budget, you mean, simply to research the Christmas party?'

'Nearly lunchtime,' said Anne.
'Can I fetch you anything from Pret?'

'Yes,' said Julian. 'Of course!'

'Why then did I also give you expenses?' Rupert asked. 'What was that for?'

Julian opened his mouth and looked up at the ceiling. Then he looked back down at his cousin, and closed his mouth.

'So, tell me. How much of that . . . first, *separate* research budget remains?' asked Rupert.

'Well . . .' Julian swallowed. 'We've done the research, haven't we? We've researched very thoroughly.'

Rupert nodded. 'None of it.'

'Not *none* of it,' said Julian. Then he remembered that, checking the budget on the way to work this morning, and seeing that some remained, he had stopped at Patisserie Valerie and, feeling very pleased with himself, had bought a cheesecake for the team – the last crumbs of which now decorated their workspaces.

'Actually, now I think of it,' he said, 'that's right. None.'

In another first for him, Rupert seemed genuinely stumped for anything to say.

'But,' pleaded Julian, 'how could we possibly organize a party for the whole company for fifteen hundred quid? In London? It just isn't feasible!'

'That's exactly why I hired *you*,' Rupert said. 'Four creative, diligent, resourceful individuals like yourselves. That was the puzzle you were supposed to crack. After all, the reason this company is in this pickle in the first place is because we're so short of money.' He was now standing by his desk, where a light had started to blink. He snatched up the desk phone and barked, 'Not now, Ricardo!' then slapped it back down.

'We're very sorry, Rupert,' said Anne.

It was extremely hard to be angry with Anne, or at least, once angry, to remain so for long. She was the very picture of angelic innocence. Even Rupert's ill temper could not hold out against her apology.

'It can't be helped,' he said. 'We'll have to put a brave face on it, and make do. I will personally put forward some of my own money to make it possible . . .'

'Sorry about this,' said Dick, looking at his shoes. 'We're all to blame.'

'Yeah, it seems sort of rough,' said George. 'The last thing we wanted to do was ruin the party . . .'

'Leave it with us,' said Julian, relieved at this more conciliatory tone. 'We'll bring you the best damned cheapskate office party of all time!'

'Well,' said Rupert. 'I certainly hope so.'

'Woof,' said George quietly, feeling that's what Timmy would have said.

CHAPTER TEN

Research and Destroy

It was extremely loyal of Dick to claim equal responsibility for the group over the budget fiasco, for they all knew it was not the case. In fact, during the weeks leading up to the report, Julian had discovered a new talent for rationalization. He managed to convince himself nearly everything he wanted, or was obliged to pay for, could be said to be in research for the Christmas party.

This included his morning coffee, several packets of Maltesers, a pair of trousers, a trip to the National Theatre, an ironing board, a subscription to the *London Review of Books* and a copy of *The LEGO Batman movie* (although, it's fair to note that the housemates had watched this together, and all enjoyed it enormously).

Julian had also comprehensively researched any restaurant that took his fancy (his definition of 'restaurant' including the fast-food concessions at London railway terminuses), as well as a couple of dozen pubs. In fact, by the time the budget ran out, he was rather glad of the fact, owing to all the weight he was putting on – the proof of which being he was already too large to fit into the trousers he had bought just a fortnight earlier.

Deep down, they probably accepted group culpability because if they had given it a second's thought, any one of them could have pointed out that being given expenses meant that the budget was not to be touched. But Julian had taken charge so quickly and with such evident delight that they had not thought to question his (in retrospect thoroughly questionable) thought processes.

So they all felt guilty – and were all very alive to the fact that there was a task still to do. The five (Timmy was in the office these days, discreetly curled up in the warm space next to the photocopier) were so mortified at their failure so far that they were determined to create a memorable party.

They were now working away at party ideas night and day, much harder than before. Except now it was on ideas that involved next to no money.

Meanwhile, life in the office progressed as usual. There was one conversation in particular that the Kirrin cousins tried to avoid, but which, to their discomfort, they found themselves having with increasing frequency.

One morning, when Dick was in the kitchen brewing the

*The board games that were dotted around on
desks disguised with picnic blankets quickly proved
to be a popular diversion.*

coffee, Helen came in. The fact that it was Helen immediately put him at a disadvantage, but the conversation that followed made him feel even more awkward.

'I'm *so* glad you guys are organizing the Christmas party,' said Helen. 'It's such a relief.'

'Oh, good,' said Dick.

'It's usually so awful,' she said. 'Just drinks in the office, as though we don't spend enough time in this place, and you get stuck in the corner talking to people who . . . who are *nice* and everything, but who you . . . just don't want to . . . you know.'

'Yeah,' said Dick. 'Yeah.'

'And everyone drinks too much, and no one can look at each other for weeks afterwards . . .'

'Huh,' said Dick. 'Yeah.'

It was very hard to talk to Helen. She was gentle and softly spoken, with silken auburn hair that fell past her shoulders in waves. She had tanned skin and soulful brown eyes, and didn't seem to walk but instead to sort of flow through the air.

Dick found it almost impossible to speak when she was around – she made him feel clumsy and stupid. Julian didn't even try. Whenever she appeared he went pink and fled from the room. Even George, never a chatterbox, went noticeably quiet. And Anne found that she simply did not warm to the girl, and always discovered she had something important to do when Helen was around, such as examining her nails with a supercilious expression.

This seemed frankly rather hard on Helen, seeing as the four housemates were the only people in the office (aside from Ken) who were roughly her age. But there was nothing to be done – she was simply too pure and ethereal. And, quite frankly, hot.

'Don't worry,' Dick lied. 'Ours won't be like that.'

'Oh, *good*,' said Helen. 'I'm so grateful you guys are in charge of it . . .'

With an elegant tilt of her chin, she gave Dick a smile which hit him like a shovel to the back of the head. Then she turned and without seeming to move, rippled into the distance and vanished like a mirage.

When Dick got back to his desk, he handed out the coffees. Julian looked at his with open distrust and placed it at arm's length, deciding that, rather than risk anything, this morning he was happy just to smell it.

'Any news on the R.R.P.?' Anne asked. 'What's the goss?'

'Rupert's plan is working,' Dick said. 'All they're talking about is the Christmas party. And how confident they are that we're going to get it right.'

'That's what I'm hearing too,' said George.

The others looked pained.

'Woof,' said Timmy. Dick chucked him one of the pastries he'd half-inched from the trolley on its way to the weekly acquisition meeting, and Timmy wolfed it noisily.

'We'd better get on, then,' said Julian. 'We're going to do this. We're going to succeed. I'm a confident businessman. Confident. Not a worm. *Not* a worm.'

'You're saying that out loud,' said George, 'bee tee dubs.'

'*Shin*splints,' said Julian.

CHAPTER ELEVEN

Christmas Party Prep

With only nine workdays to go until the big day, which was the 16th December, the four housemates gathered at one of the break-out spaces to share their final ideas.

'Hit me!' said Julian.

They hit him.

It soon emerged that their recent embarrassment had sharpened their intellects. Horrified at the prospect of ruining the party for their innocent colleagues, they had focused to the best of their abilities – with the result that they were pleasantly surprised to find they liked each other's ideas. Even better, many of their suggestions dovetailed with each other. There was very little discussion – within a few minutes, they had a firm plan.

The office Christmas party was to be on a theme of austerity. Not a mean and spartan one, however, but one that looked back wistfully to the 1940s.

'A more innocent time,' said Anne.

'Except for the Second World War, of course,' Dick said.

'And the Holocaust,' said George.

'And millions starving and being purged in Russia,' said Julian.

'For pity's sake, Julian, you're supposed to be on my side!' said Anne. 'A *more innocent time*,' she doggedly repeated, 'full of wholesome activities, and fun, and games, which will remind everyone of childhood.'

'Great stuff,' said Julian. 'I love it.'

'Scrumping?' asked George.

'*Scrumping*,' agreed Anne.

'Bunting?' asked Dick.

'Bunting!' Anne insisted.

'Can someone say something that doesn't rhyme, please?' asked Julian. He looked at his pad. 'How about pass the parcel? And musical chairs?'

'Those board games in the pub gave me an idea,' said Anne. 'How about snakes and ladders, and so on? Guess Who? Hungry Hippos?'

'Mousetrap!' said Julian.

'Duck, duck, goose?' suggested Anne.

'I don't know about all this,' said Dick. 'Will people go along with it?'

'I think they might, you know,' said George. 'Sometimes you get tired of being a hardened and cynical adult living in

London. Playing some nice innocent games – I think people might find it refreshing. Honestly.'

'Me too,' said Julian. 'I think it's a master stroke. In fact, do you know, I think I'm glad I blew all that cash . . .'

'Don't push your bloody luck,' said Anne.

Food was agreed on: pies, sandwiches, sausage rolls, Scotch eggs (quiche was mentioned, but immediately shouted down). Cake, trifle, jelly and ice cream. Drink, too: teapots filled with punch, a tea urn filled with cider. They also included a list of soft drinks, for hypothetical abstainers.

'I can't believe we've actually nailed this,' said Julian. 'What can we make at home in the flat to save even more money?'

'Lots and lots,' said Anne. 'I'll do the bunting, and hunt in charity shops for the board games.'

'Brilliant,' said Dick. 'I think they'll actually feel better if the sets don't look brand new.'

'I'll do the sandwiches,' said Julian. 'I've got a full hip flask full of Noilly Prat and a Wilkie Collins audiobook. That should get me through a few hundred rounds of spam on white.'

'I can make a trifle,' said Dick.

They all turned to yell at him for being silly. Everyone knew his culinary repertoire extended no further than the

*As the scent from the punchbowl reached him,
Timmy whimpered and retreated into the darkness.*

sausage sandwich. But then they paused, recollecting that, after they had made the same complaint a few years earlier, he had proved them wrong by making a perfectly decent trifle – rather good, in fact.

'Step up to the plate and make two,' said Julian.

'I'll make three,' said Dick, 'if you promise never to say "step up to the plate" again.'

'Knock it out of the park, and I'll consider it,' said Julian. 'Bonza! Good work, team!'

'Woof!' said Timmy.

'*Sssssssshhhhhhh*,' said everyone else, looking around the office guiltily.

CHAPTER TWELVE

The Party Arrives

There was nothing the five liked more than an adventure. Which this now most definitely was. With a plan to work to, and an end in sight, they really started to enjoy themselves.

Rupert approved the plan at once, as they'd known he must, because it was such a jolly good plan. He was also clearly surprised and grateful for the extra personal effort they were pledging. After leaving his office, they began preparations at once.

They shopped and they carried and they cut and they sewed; they cooked and they buttered and they iced and they sliced. They made each other cups of tea and they nibbled the occasional sandwich or teacake or piece of chocolate biscuit cake that was supposed to be for the party, just to keep themselves going. They worked long after midnight every night. Then, with the day almost upon them, they bagged and they boxed and they taped and they carried.

By the night before the party they were exhausted, but glowing with pride.

'Take a sip of that little bad boy,' said Julian, holding out a ladle.

'Sweet Christmas pudding up the backside,' said Dick, 'that's got a bit of a *phhrrrr*.' He lost his breath as the astonishingly pungent flavour gave way to an eye-wateringly concentrated aftertaste.

'Hah!' said Julian. 'Welcome to Elsinore, Horatio. We'll teach you to drink deep ere you depart!'

'Yeah, well, now I know why everyone dies at the end of that play,' said Dick. 'Seriously, aren't you supposed to water it down a bit? If you serve that up, there'll be a riot!'

'Nonsense – you're just out of practice,' said Julian. 'Besides, I'm not changing the recipe now – I've just made three hundred rounds of corned-beef sandwiches and I'm dead on my feet. I'm going to bottle this magic up and bung myself off to bed.'

Dick eyed his brother darkly as he retreated. But, after thirteen trips to Lidl and back, and emptying or at least heavily depleting their stock of pork pies, piccalilli, English mustard, napkins, paper cups, paper plates, orange squash and a few dozen other items, Dick was too tired to argue.

Besides, that sip of punch had already gone to his head. He went off to sleep.

The following morning there was a nervous energy in the air. A seemingly interminable number of car trips to the office finally got everything there, and hour after hour of laying things out finally got the office party space looking ready.

'Amazing,' said Julian, standing back and looking at it. 'Looks great! And just in time for the party to begin! I can't believe you managed to get hold of hay bales, Dick – a masterful touch.'

They really had managed to make a great long span of office look like a 1940s picnic spot – if one overlooked the filing cabinets and office machinery, which one could just about do, after the dimming of the lights (which involved Dick removing eighty per cent of the bulbs and nearly being electrocuted three times).

'Hey, who normally works in this office?' asked George. 'Why aren't they here today?'

'R.R.P.,' said Ken morosely.

George jumped.

'Don't creep up on me!' she said. 'But still, it's nice to see you. You're the first guest. Cup of punch? There's a forty per cent chance it will make you go blind.'

'That's inviting,' said Ken. 'But I'll start with cider, for choice.'

'Sure thing,' said George. Like the others, she instinctively warmed to Ken. 'Hey, play a game with me? We've got Battleships.'

'How enchanting,' said Ken. 'I can't imagine anything making me happier.'

'Newsflash,' said George. 'Play Battleships with me and enjoy it, or I'll kidney-punch you.'

'The very words which sealed the betrothal of the young Victoria and Prince Albert,' said Ken. 'I accept.'

'That's the spirit.'

Office workers drifted down to the party slowly, at first. There was music – of course there was music – but George had rather brilliantly curated a mixture of trad jazz, early rock 'n' roll and sweet Dennis Potter/Ink Spots-era ballads that everyone liked. Gradually the corners of the room started to fill up, and a few people began playing games at the tables.

There was laughter, and playful shouting. People were drinking cider. Anne and Dick buzzed around offering people food from plates while Julian stood at the door, welcoming people, explaining what to find and where, and casting anxious looks around the room.

Jim Granger arrived, lurked at the door to share an

Dick and George were possessed by a sudden energy to
get everyone out of the building.

extremely dirty joke with Julian, whom he called Dick, laughed alone while ignoring Julian's horrified stare, told Julian he was 'all right, son', grabbed three sandwiches off a passing tray and walked off.

Suze arrived.

'Eighteen and a half years old,' she said, 'and she's got herpes.'

'Who?' asked Julian, looking round.

'My daughter!'

'This is a night of celebration,' said Julian, with dignity. 'Let us leave herpes out of it, insofar as possible.'

'I suppose you're right,' said Suze. 'Where's the plonk?'

'We've got four types of cider circling on trays with my glamorous assistants, Anne and Dick,' said Julian. 'Fill your boots.'

'You'll be all right, my love,' said Suze, 'but I don't fancy Anne's chances, with this R.R.P. She's a suck-up, you see? They don't respect that, the up-aboves. They'll move her to the basement, if she's lucky – and they've had two suicides down there this month here she comes . . . *Hiiiiiiii*, Anne, my darling girl. You look so *niiiiice*. How d'you *do* it?'

'I'm not sure what it is that I do,' said Anne nicely, 'but I'm glad you think I'm doing it.'

Suze nodded, not listening, and grasping Anne's elbow,

escorted her away. Without checking they were out of Julian's earshot, she said, 'Listen, don't tell anyone, but Julian's definitely going, under the R.R.P. . . .'

Julian watched them both disappear into the crowd.

'Jesus Christ eating a watermelon,' he said. 'What a horrible woman.'

'JULIAN,' said a voice three inches from his left ear.

Julian's spine wriggled like an eel as he tried to prevent himself performing a somersault.

'Rupert,' he said. 'You came.'

'Can't stay long,' Rupert said. 'But, I must say, you all pulled it out of the bag. You've really pulled it out of the bag.'

'I suppose you could say that we stepped up to the plate and knocked it out of the park,' Julian suggested.

'*You* might,' said Rupert. 'I personally find phrases like that rather irritating.'

'Right-ho,' said Julian. 'Well, there's cider and pies and whatnot. And jolly games. Good clean fun, all round.'

'Great stuff. You've thought outside the box,' said Rupert.

'Ha!' said Julian, although, from his expression, it wasn't at all clear Rupert was joking. 'Hey, Rupert,' he said, catching his cousin by the sleeve. 'When are you going to tell these guys what's going on? And where they stand, with regards to their jobs? They're terrified. They're just people, Rupert. It's ruining their lives.'

'It's a difficult process,' said Rupert, 'but it has to be done properly. When the project is complete, it will be complete.'

'Classic Rupert,' whispered Julian, as Rupert oozed away into the crowd.

Julian watched as a tall, sunken-eyed man walked forward. Despite his height, he stooped, and glanced around with a hunted look.

'Hullo, Penny,' said Julian.

'Hi,' said Ian Penny. 'Is he here?'

'Yeah, just went in ahead of you. Went thataway.'

Penny wrinkled his nose. 'I'll go in the opposite direction, then; find myself a cider.'

'Hey, Ian. Why does he call you Penny, when no one else does?'

'Apart from you, you mean? Because he knows I hate it, I suspect.'

'Huh. Sorry to hear that,' said Julian. 'Hey, Ian, while you're here. Can you point out Rog to me? Ken hinted there was something distinctive about his appearance, but refused to say what it was.'

Ian Penny did so.

'Ah,' said Julian. 'Oh. Yes. Oh dear. Well, anyway, er, do

have an enjoyable evening, Penny.' Julian patted him on the back as he walked away.

'Oh, my,' said Helen, laughing.

Julian's insides turned into spaghetti. He hiccupped.

'What's in store, Julian?' she asked.

'Lots,' said Julian, with masterful self-control. 'Games – picnic food – party atmosphere – drinks – nostalgia. Something for everyone.'

'Oh, goody. You are clever. What fun!' she said, and wafted away. Julian put his hand against the wall for support.

'Woof?' enquired Timmy from beneath a nearby table.

'Indeed,' said Julian. 'Couldn't have put it better myself.'

CHAPTER THIRTEEN

Not-So-Secret Santa

The board games that were dotted around on desks disguised with picnic blankets quickly proved to be a popular diversion. In the centre of the room, Anne and Julian supervised the scrumping and the musical chairs, which passed off with much energy and laughter, and without any notable controversy.

Then the music was turned down and, seeing her signal, Anne clapped for everyone's attention.

'Now it's time for someone very special to visit us,' she said. 'A person who holds a unique place in all our hearts at this time of year . . .'

In the absence of a spotlight, Julian turned an Anglepoise lamp towards a nearby open door.

Everyone tensed and leant forward, wondering who this could possibly be. A stripper? Surely not. A music act? Please, no. What, then?

There was the sound of a slight scuffle, and someone saying, 'But I don't bloody want to!' to which came the answer, 'You owe me big time, you bastard; now, get out there.' There was an exclamation of pain, roughly equivalent in severity to a man being kicked hard in the backside, and then a figure appeared in the doorway. He looked at the crowd grumpily and belched.

'Ho ho ho?' he asked.

A cheer went up that clearly startled the man.

To the assembled employees, his costume clearly identified him as Santa Claus. To the four housemates and Timmy, however, his voice, eyes, pipe-tobacco smell and habit of nervous belching identified him as Uncle Quentin.

'I hope you've all been, er . . .' He rummaged in his pocket, pulled out a scrap of paper, and held it away from his head while adjusting his glasses. 'Jesus Christ,' he muttered. Then he looked up from the paper and said more loudly, '. . . good boys and girls?'

Everyone cheered, louder than before.

Rather in opposition to Uncle Quentin's intentions, his grumpy performance was going down very well with this mildly cider-happy crowd. They were under the impression that he was a comedian performing in character, and from now on nothing he could say dissuaded them. He was already getting titters from around the room.

'All right, let's get this over with,' he sighed. 'If you

Everyone tensed and leaned forward, wondering
who this new arrival could be. A stripper? Surely not.
A music act? Please, no.

have all been good little boys and girls, or however you self-identify, as my daughter insists I point out, then please step forward one by one to receive your Secret Santa present!'

At the mention of presents, was an even louder cheer.

'Get in a bloody queue; don't rush me,' Santa said, picking his nose. 'I don't want to have another heart attack.'

The workers had already formed an orderly queue. As the music was turned back up, Dick and George serviced their happily queuing colleagues with further cups of cider.

'I think it's going well,' said Julian. 'Is Rupert still here?'

'God, no,' said Anne. 'He went round the room once, practically at a sprint, and then scarpered. But I agree, people do seem to be enjoying themselves.'

'After this, I think the night should really get going,' said Julian. 'George has some slightly funkier music cued up and I'm going to break out the punch.'

Anne put a hand on his arm.

'I'm really not sure about that punch, Julian . . .' she said.

'Oh, stuff and non-science,' he said. 'You're fake noose! Get out of here. I've had some, and I'm all right.'

'You practically run on alcohol,' said Anne, with unusual directness, 'and it's more or less blitzed you. You're weaving from side to side and I even saw you having a conversation with that Helen, just now.'

'Don't call her "*that Helen*",' said Julian, with hauteur, 'like she's committed some sort of crime. She's a lovely girl, if you make the effort to get to know her.'

Anne scoffed. 'I've seen her sort before. It's all an act.'

'Now, Anne, don't misunderstand her . . .' slurred Julian, as they walked away.

Thus it was that Anne allowed herself to be distracted from the topic of the punch. And, lacking the crucial investigation of a sober party, it was allowed to become available for general consumption.

Timmy, meanwhile, who did not enjoy all the shouting and laughter in this strange dark room one whit, had come to lie next to a large tea urn filled with Julian's punch. Settling down for a light doze, a wisp of its fumes trickled over him, and connected with his nose.

'Woof!'

He jumped up, on guard at this suspicious smell. He sniffed, and sniffed again, and then whimpered and retreated into the shadows, with considerably less than his usual canine agility.

CHAPTER FOURTEEN

The Party Gets into Full Swing

The four housemates noticed that the noise in the room had, over the course of a few minutes, suddenly grown much louder. They could hardly hear themselves think.

There was a scuffle in the middle of the room, and, rushing over, they found it was Ian Penny and Jon Granger, fighting. Jon Granger had pulled Ian's jacket up over his head to disable him, and Ian was grappling him to prevent him having the room to swing.

Dick and Julian pulled the two apart. There was a lot of screaming and throwing of air punches, and after appearing becalmed Ian twice launched himself back at his assailant with furious energy, nearly breaking through the group restraining him.

'SAY THAT AGAIN!' he screamed. 'JUST SAY THAT AGAIN, YOU—'

'Calm down, calm down,' Julian shouted in his ear. 'Here. Sit down.'

'Don't let him near me,' said Ian, from the chair where

they'd placed him. Various colleagues gathered round, telling him to forget it, and that it was not worth it, and that he was a better man if he didn't rise to it, even though none of them knew what 'it' was.

'What is going *on*?' Anne asked the others, when the fight seemed under control. She shouted, in fact, as this was the only way to be heard.

'I think they've tasted the punch,' said Julian.

'What did you *put* in there?' George asked. 'Did you follow a recipe?'

'I don't follow recipes,' Julian yelled scornfully, 'I vibe it, mate! Plenty of booze, and top it off with punch.'

The others waited for him to make some sign that this was a joke. He did not.

'Punch isn't a mixer, Julian,' said Anne.

'Of course it is!'

'It bloody isn't,' said George.

'Have you never drunk it before?' Anne asked.

'Well, no . . . but I don't have to—'

'Julian,' shouted Anne crossly, 'punch is the alcohol part. You're supposed to water it down with lemonade and stuff – not spice it up with extra booze!'

'So there's no mixer in it *at all*?' Dick asked.

'There's lots of fruit,' Julian said.

THE PARTY GETS INTO FULL SWING

At that moment, they were interrupted by a crash as Megs Smith from Special Sales, daubed with war paint, leapt hollering from a desk with the intention of crowd surfing. They helped her to a side room, mopped up the blood, administered first aid, and asked her if she knew who the prime minister was, and if she could name the day of the week. Then they lay her on a sofa, under a blanket.

It was all so stressful that Julian fetched each of them cups of punch to help them deal with it, and soon enough they felt they had everything under control.

'It's moreish in its own peculiar, horrible way,' said George. 'You are to be congraptubaytig. Congrangerlay . . .'

Anne hiccuped.

Dick put his hand to his head.

'Hey, guys,' came a voice from the door. It was Ron from Sales, looking insane. 'We're going to hide all the keyboards in the whole building.'

'That sounds . . .' Anne said disapprovingly. She ran out of words and her head nodded for a while. Then she seemed to snap to attention. '*Where* are we going to hide them?' she asked.

'In here, in here,' whispered Dick. 'This must be the place.'

There was much giggling as Dick, George, Anne and a

bunch of others dragged heavy bin liners down the corridor. They had stolen all the keyboards from every PC in the building (except from Rupert's office, which was locked) and were now looking for the most secretive and inconvenient place to hide them.

Julian, whose alcoholic intake was a good deal further along than the others, had insisted that they put them in the skip outside. But the others wanted to hide rather than destroy company property, and, in protest at his suggestion not being taken up, Julian had lain down in the skip to sleep.

The others had ventured into the basement, a place of whirring and blinking servers, mysterious doors and blank, featureless passageways that led no one knew where. Two-thirds of the way down the central corridor, Dick got tired of hauling his sack and, selecting the nearest door, threw it open.

Dick and his partners in crime all gasped.

The inhabitants of the room screamed.

'What is happening here?' shrieked Anne.

'Jesus Christ in a hockey mask!' shouted Dick.

Inside was a caretaker's room, in the middle of which was a large boiler. The boiler was not, however, the cause of Dick and Anne's complaint. It was the two people immediately behind it, who were hurrying to separate themselves.

Under the ministrations of Timmy's affection, George's face looked like it was going through a car wash.

'Mind your own business!' shouted Ken, reaching for his trousers.

'We've all got needs, *Dick*,' said Suze, covering herself with her skirt and casting him and the onlookers with a lascivious stare.

Dick leapt away down the corridor with a yell. Everyone else was dumbstruck, but followed him to escape the sight they had just set eyes upon (although little hoping there was any chance they would forget it in a hurry).

Desperate to maintain the momentum of fun and humour of the prank, Dick reached for the next door he came across in the corridor, and swung it open.

This time Dick didn't even make a noise, but covered his eyes and ran away.

'I see you two got over your differences,' said George, lolling in the doorway.

'Could we have some privacy?' asked Jim Granger, looking round.

'*Please*?' asked Ian Penny, yanking his trousers up.

George sighed, and pulled the door shut.

The group staggered along now, feeling sobered and resenting the weight of the sacks they carried behind them. There was only one door left for them to go through, at the end of the corridor. By now, they were all much too drunk to admit that this was the one room in the building they had always feared above all.

Finding it locked, and having no intention of turning back and explaining themselves to any of the people they had just bumped into, the group discovered a new, daring energy. They gathered themselves, and ran at the door with all their energy, attempting to barge it en masse.

The corridor was filled with pitiful cries of pain. Then, a second later, it was again.

But the door gave at the third try.

They staggered into a large, dark space. Dick flipped the light switch, but it didn't work. With drunken curiosity, they all spread out to investigate what appeared to be an underground warehouse filled with items and boxes on shelves.

'This reminds me,' Dick said. 'I've never thought to ask. What do we actually do in this company?'

'Special Sales,' said Megs Smith, who, with a bandage over one eye, was stumbling into things.

'But what is Special Sales?' asked George. 'What do we sell, specially or otherwise?'

'Special things,' came Megs' voice. 'Ow!' she said, tripping over something.

There was a row with a sign at one end that read *PROJECT X*. There was another which announced itself as *OPERATION*

DARKFORCE, and for a moment George was sure she saw the phrase *EL CHAPO* over what looked like a cache of hardware, just before the torchlight from her phone cut out.

Dick was at that moment searching down an adjacent aisle, at the end of which, he saw, was a blackboard covered with photos and names, with many of them crossed out, but all connected by a web of lines. Dick had just noticed there was a headline reading *CARTEL LEFTOVERS*, when he was distracted by voices from a few feet away.

'It's amazing how convincing these replicas are, isn't it?' Anne said.

'I'd put that down, Anne,' said George.

'Look at all these parcels of white powder,' said Anne. 'And brown ones too. So we sell . . . sugar, right? Oh, look, I pressed a button on this box and now it's ticking. What's it for, do you think? It feels too heavy to be a toy.'

'Put it down!' said George.

'Bomb alert!' Dick said. 'It's definitely time to go home! Follow me!'

'Woof!' said Timmy.

'Timmy! What are *you* doing here?' George shouted. 'Let's skedaddle!'

CHAPTER FIFTEEN

Exit Wounds

Dick and George were possessed by a sudden energy to get everyone out of the building. To their great relief, they found that the two basement store cupboards they had recently entered were now empty. But there was much more to do, and fast.

Dick rushed upstairs, switched off the music, turned on what lights remained, and then directed the blinking drunkards out on to the street to gather together at the fire-assembly point on the opposite pavement. He made a last quick sweep of the rooms they'd been in, and then, remembering, grabbed Julian from the skip beside the building.

'What?' Julian protested as Dick dragged him to safety. 'What is this? Why on earth are you being so—'

The last word in the sentence was lost beneath a loud boom.

Julian turned woozily to follow everyone else's gaze. There was a second explosion, another almost immediately after, and then a cluster of them, all seeming to emanate from the basement.

'What the devil's going—' asked Anne. But she was cut off by a rumble beneath their feet, and the sound of hundreds of windows shattering.

Dust billowed up from the basement, ballooning to fill the street, and simultaneously the building's roof started to sink. The rumbling grew in intensity until the roof vanished down into the expanding dust cloud.

George dimly realised that in the wholesale physical destruction of the office, she was witnessing her fantasy coming true. She knew she ought to be grateful, but for some reason it wasn't quite as satisfying as she'd expected.

Sirens could already be heard in the distance.

'So he *didn't* have to test the fire alarm every morning,' Julian muttered and, turning his dust-covered face to Dick, shouted something that sounded vaguely like, 'The fire alarm didn't work. We should go!'

'What?' asked Dick, his ears ringing.

Anne grabbed his arm. He turned to her and, from reading her lips, thought he made out the words '. . . make ourselves scarce.'

'Say again?' yelled Dick.

'They do have sports bras in Austria, you know.'

He was suddenly yanked off his feet as George gripped him by the lapels.

'What is it?' he asked.

'LET'S SCRAM!' she said.

'Woof!' came a voice, from somewhere in the dust cloud.

CHAPTER SIXTEEN

A New Life

The sky was a bright, clear blue. Gulls could be heard on the wind, only serving to emphasise the village's very picture of stillness.

A little old man wearing dark glasses climbed the road with slow, deliberate steps. He was making his way towards a humble restaurant on the crest of the hill. Watching him from the tables outside was a buxom Austrian girl in blonde pigtails and traditional dress, who was feeding table scraps to a local mountain goat that had dared to come near. At another table was a nun, gently blowing the steam off a cup of herbal tea.

The old man at last attained the top of the hill, where he stopped for a few breaths to admire the view. It was stunning. The Mediterranean Sea stretched out gloriously in every direction, and the sharp January wind was blunted by the bright winter sun. Taking in the view, the old man inhaled a deep, satisfying breath.

Then he hobbled over and sat gingerly at one of the

chairs outside the café. A waiter came out to take his order, and briskly disappeared. The old man sighed, and smiled beatifically. The nun and the Austrian woman both cast him sympathetic glances.

He turned slowly towards the nun, who was nearest him.

'I say,' he said. 'Pardon me. Speak the English?'

The nun nodded encouragingly.

'Wonderful winter weather,' he said.

'I wonder if it is so bright,' the nun replied, 'in London?'

'Anne! It *is* you!' said George, whipping her dark glasses off. Then she hurriedly replaced them as the waiter returned with her caffè latte. '*Obrigado*,' she said hurriedly. '*Danke, danke*!'

The nun had already leapt up to join him at his table. She looked over her shoulder. She saw the mountain goat was suddenly straining at the leash by which it was tied to a nearby wooden post.

'Woof!' it said. 'Woof, woof!'

As the Austrian woman struggled to untangle its lead, the goat suddenly gained its freedom and overturned her table as it leapt towards the old man, whose face it covered with friendly licks.

'Oh, there you are, my special boy, my special man, my little lad, you special thing,' George said, grabbing Timmy

'Woof!' yelled Timmy, begging to be included. A few seconds later, they were all sitting around the table, telling of their journeys.

in a big hug, and kissing him. 'God, you're sweaty. You've really ruined my face make-up. Has Aunty Julian kept you in this costume all week?'

'Woof!' said Timmy. 'Woof!'

'Do you think this was all really necessary?' Anne asked, looking down at her nun's costume and lamenting that it hid all of the parts of her that she liked best. 'I mean, did we really all have to come all the way to Corsica, and by different routes?'

'It depends,' George said, blinking quickly, as, under the ministrations of Timmy's effusive greeting, her face looked like it was going through a carwash. 'When escaping from a murderous cartel, do you take the easiest route and trust you'll be okay, or do you take the utmost measures to ensure your security?'

'Woof!' said Timmy. 'Woof, woof!'

'I love you too,' said George. 'Now, quiet, Mr Goat, or you'll get us spotted. We're undercover, remember?'

'Waaaaaaa,' said Timmy, 'Whuhuhuhuhuh-aaaaa!'

Everyone covered their ears.

'Very convincing, Robert De Niro,' said George. 'Take it over there, won't you, so the rest of us can talk?'

'I've no idea how you deal with having these things on

the front of your chest all the time,' said Julian, the Austrian maid, lumbering over. 'They go all over the place!'

'Only if they're utterly enormous, like your ones,' said George. 'They do have sports bras in Austria, you know.'

'I like your pigtails,' said Anne.

'Yes,'. said Julian. 'Me too! They're rather pretty. These norks, though – nightmare. I kept getting them caught in tram doors!'

At that moment they were arrested by a sound they had all been aware of for some time, but which had suddenly got louder. It was a rhythmic metal creak. They turned and saw a clown, in full costume and make-up, cycling up the hill towards them. There was a painted smile which stretched almost up to his eyes, but at a second glance one saw that his face was actually set in a grimace of pain. He was gasping for breath.

They all leapt to their feet.

'Hello, Dick!' they all shouted.

The clown fell off his bike, and tumbled into a hedge. He clambered out of it with his wig in his hands, from which he spent a few moments extracting leaves. Then he looked up at them anxiously. '*Scusa*?' he asked.

'Oh, hi, guys,' said a voice behind them.

They turned to see the tall, handsome waiter. He took off

They all quickly settled into a going-to-work routine.

his fake eyebrows – and Dick was himself again. They threw themselves at him in a big hug.

'Woof!' yelled Timmy, begging to be included. A few seconds later, they were all sitting around the table, telling of their journeys.

'So sad to miss a Christmas at home,' Anne asked. 'And not to have a stocking to empty.'

'Balls to that,' said George, 'I'd rather miss a few presents than risk being at the bottom of a reservoir somewhere. Do you think we're safe, Julian?'

'It's impossible to say,' said Julian. 'There's nothing more we can do. We have exposed and angered a whole clique of important international gangs and there will be a bounty on our heads. It's a miracle we made it this far. Now we must begin our lives as humble turf-cutters . . .'

His voice trailed away as a car glided to a halt beside their table. It was clean, expensive and new, with darkened windows. They gazed at it with undisguised terror.

A door opened on the other side and a man stepped out, shaven headed and deeply tanned. He walked round towards them slowly. He wore a faded black suit, chauffeur's gloves and dark glasses. The suit jacket bulged with huge muscles in the chest and arms, but his face was spread with the leathery wrinkles of a man well into his sixties. He moved with the perfect grace of a robot.

Julian grabbed a fork off the table and leapt up, brandishing it.

'Stay back! This isn't the end! I'll take you with me!'

Dick was better prepared. Reaching around to the small of his back, he produced a meat cleaver. He crouched, and weaved from left to right, throwing the cleaver from one hand to the other and back, his waiter's apron flapping in the mountain wind.

'Wanna dance?' he asked.

The man placed a briefcase on the table facing the group, and popped it open. Within, lying flat and surrounded by protective foam, was a tablet. As they looked at it, it tilted up to face them.

The housemates all looked at the chauffeur, but he remained utterly unimpressible behind his dark glasses. So they looked back at the screen. It was black for a moment, then a video started playing.

Rupert appeared, sitting in an armchair behind an enormous varnished desk made from dark wood. He was in some sort of library.

'*Dear* cousins,' he said, leaning back in his leather chair.

'It has come to my attention that, for reasons unknown, you fear retribution for some act or other.'

'How did he *find* us?' screamed Julian.

'Woof!' agreed Timmy.

'Shhh,' said Anne.

'If you're wondering how I found you,' said Rupert, 'then don't. It's easier than do-re-mi to track people in the modern world, to be honest. Especially if they log on to their account to play *Pokémon GO* in Madrid, Dick, or order a very specific brand of English dog food from a shop in Marseilles, George, or angrily demand in English to be moved to the Quiet Carriage when boarding the Orient Express – especially while dressed as a large-breasted nineteenth-century Austrian peasant woman, Julian.'

Julian jealously clutched his protrusions.

'Or if they simply look like you, Anne,' Rupert went on. 'I wish I could have saved all of you the trouble of this elaborate vanishing act. For, you see, it was not in the least necessary. What you thought I was seeking to conceal, I was in fact intending to expose. Why do you think I would invite the four of you—'

'Woof!'

'—*five*, excuse my forgetfulness, Timmy ... Why would I invite the five of you into the company I was

'Why would I invite the five of you into the company
I was running to organize a Christmas party, unless it
was to cause mayhem and destruction?'

running to organize a Christmas party, unless it was to cause mayhem and destruction? I needed to cover my tracks and remove evidence of my contact with a variety of foreign interests. I chose to do this by instigating an accidental-seeming disaster,' Rupert said. 'And you performed *wonderfully.*'

'You beast!' cried Anne.

'Yes, Anne,' said the recording, 'I quite agree. But, to ensure you fear no reprisals from this – admittedly very ugly and threatening – messenger, I'd like to set your mind at ease. You performed your tasks admirably. I needed my tracks covered, and you did it. Although I am here in my comfortable little hideaway in the Bahamas, or the Caymans, or wherever you suppose me to be, it doesn't mean I can't give you a richly earned present. Arturo, if you would be so good. Happy Christmas bonus, cousins!'

The video stopped, and, with one gesture, the driver snapped shut the briefcase. Then he took from the inside pocket of his jacket a small navy silk pouch tied with a string. As he put it down, whatever was inside clicked invitingly. Without looking back, Arturo walked to the car, got in and drove away.

Julian fondled his fake breasts in excitement.

'What do you think it could be?' he asked. 'Shall we look? Will we be rich? And happy? At last?'

George reached over and untied the string. 'Shall I empty it out?' she asked.

'Woof!' said Timmy. 'Woof, woof!'